THE
PUPPY
TALES
COLLECTION

INTRODUCTION

I don't know if you have every visited the fine town of Houndsville. No? Well, it is home to the finest pack of dogs you could ever hope to meet—and the naughtiest puppies, too! You can meet Houndsville's most famous citizens in the stories in this book. Look out for Mr. Bones the Baker, Duchess Dulay, Dasher the Delivery Dog, and many others.

There is always something going on in Houndsville. What happened to Duchess Dulay's diamond bracelet? Was Mr. Terrier the Teacher really attacked by an alien life form? Why is Mrs. Gruff the Greengrocer so tired these days? Why was Sir Woofington Paws so pleased to meet a thief in his house?

You will soon know the answers to all these questions, and if you look very carefully at the pictures, you will find lots of hidden surprises there, as well.

Pictures tell stories too from age to age;
If you search you may spot
One bone (or a lot!)
Hidden on every page.

THE
PUPPY
TALES
COLLECTION

Illustrated by
CATHIE SHUTTLEWORTH

Written by
NICOLA BAXTER

ARMADILLO

FOR ANDREW KELLOCK
C.A.S.

© 1999 Bookmart Limited

Published by Armadillo Books
an imprint of
Bookmart Limited
Registered Number 2372865
Trading as Bookmart Limited
Desford Road
Enderby
Leicester
LE9 5AD

ISBN 1-90046-602-3

Produced for Bookmart Limited by Nicola Baxter
PO Box 71
Diss
Norfolk
IP22 2DT

Editorial consultant: Ronne Randall
Designer: Amanda Hawkes

Printed in Italy

CONTENTS

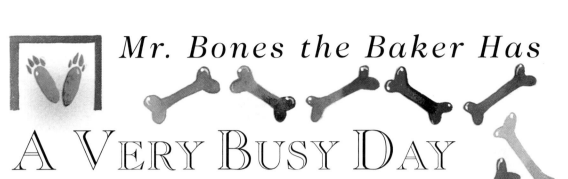

Mr. Bones the Baker Has A Very Busy Day

There are times, as I'm sure you know, when your tummy suddenly feels as empty as a bowl without a bone. You need a snack, and you need it fast. If you should happen to find yourself in Houndsville, I recommend that you trot along, as fast as your paws will carry you, to Mr. Bones the Baker's shop. You won't need to ask any of the fine dogs of the town where to find it. Just point your nose into the air and sniff. Aaaaaahhh!

Like all bakers, Mr. Bones gets up before dawn to start making the pies and pastries for which he is famous. While the streetlamps still flicker yellow in the darkness, he is going about his business, mixing and measuring, cooking and cooling. Many of the dogs in Houndsville don't bother with alarm clocks. When the fourth batch of Mr. Bones' meat pies comes out of the oven, they *know* it is time for breakfast!

Mr. Bones has baked his way through days and weeks and years, but just recently he has begun to feel too old to be up before the sun. That is why a sign appeared in his shop this morning, advertising for an assistant.

Meanwhile, Mr. Bones must struggle on by himself. After the meat pies, which are easily his most popular item, he starts working on his cakes and pastries, which include such delights as bone-marrow rolls and fish dainties. No self-respecting dog in Houndsville would dream of sitting down to afternoon tea without some of these delicacies.

One morning, just as Mr. Bones was putting the finishing touches on his iced bone-jelly jubilees, he heard a rat-a-tat-tat at the shop door. He glanced at the clock. It was only half past six.

Mr. Bones felt a bit grumpy as he wiped his paws on his apron and hurried to the door. But his manner changed as soon as he saw who was there. It was Duchess Dulay, the most glamorous dog in Houndsville, even if she was now getting on in years. To tell you the truth, Mr. Bones had quite a soft spot for the Duchess, and he sometimes had rosy dreams of sharing his retirement with her.

But today Duchess Dulay's normally perfect grooming was a little windswept and wild. She looked upset, and Mr. Bones' tender heart immediately went out to her as he undid the bolts and flung open the door.

"My dear Duchess," he cried. "Whatever is the matter?"

"Oh, Mr. Bones," said the lady. She was close to tears. "I'm so sorry to disturb you at this time of the day, but I haven't been able to get a wink of sleep all night. Do you remember yesterday, when I was in your shop buying bone buns for my tea?"

"Yes, indeed," replied Mr. Bones. "You arrived just as I was checking my flour deliveries. I do apologize if I was not able to give you my full attention. Surely the bone buns didn't give you … that is, surely there was nothing wrong with the buns?" Mr. Bones wasn't sure it was polite to mention tummy upsets to a lady.

The Duchess quickly put his mind at rest. "No, no, my dear dog," she cried. "The buns were delicious as usual. It's my diamond bracelet!"

Mr. Bones waited. He didn't have the faintest idea what she was talking about.

"I lost it, you see," said the elegant dog. "Sometime during the day, yesterday, the clasp came loose and it slipped from my wrist. It's my own silly fault. I knew that the clasp was faulty and I should have asked Miss Ruby to fix it. How I wish I had!"

"But my dear lady," said Mr. Bones with an anxious frown, "what makes you think you lost it here?"

"By a process of elimination," said Duchess Dulay grandly.

Mr. Bones' visitor soon explained that she had retraced her steps of the day before, and at every place that she had stopped, someone or other could remember seeing the very glittery and eye-catching bracelet on her wrist.

"Yes! I remember seeing it myself," cried Mr. Bones. "It is very beautiful. Oh! But that means you were definitely wearing it when you arrived."

"Yes, and I certainly wasn't when I left," said the Duchess. "Never mind how I know that. I've figured it out. Now, let's do a thorough search for it. It can't have gone far."

And much to Mr. Bones' distress, the grand lady got down on her paws and started searching vigorously under the shelves and the counter.

"Wait! Please wait!" cried Mr. Bones. "It simply can't be there! I sweep the shop very carefully every evening before I close up. I can assure you that I would have noticed a diamond bracelet. I pride myself on keeping the shop spotless."

Duchess Dulay straightened up, a little pink in the face. "Of course you do, Mr. Bones," she said. "I didn't mean to suggest otherwise. But where can the bracelet have gone?"

At just the same moment, the same awful thought came to both Mr. Bones and his visitor.

"The flour sacks!" she cried. "They were open so you could check them. The bracelet must have slipped inside!"

And without another word, she marched through the shop and straight to the back where the ovens were. "Where is the flour?" she cried. "Where do you store it?"

Mr. Bones waved his paw at the trays and trays of pies, cakes, and pastries that covered every surface.

"I don't," he said simply. "I don't store it, I use it. All the flour that arrived yesterday has been made into the things you see before you. The bracelet must be *inside* one of these!"

There was an awful silence, as both dogs looked hopelessly around. Then Mr. Bones sprang into action.

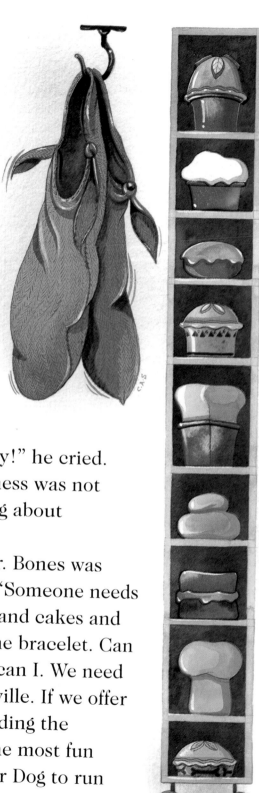

"What we need is a street party!" he cried.

"Really, Mr. Bones!" The Duchess was not amused. "How can you be thinking about frivolities at a time like this?"

For the first time in his life, Mr. Bones was rather blunt with Duchess Dulay. "Someone needs to munch and chew all those pies and cakes and pastries," he said, "until we find the bracelet. Can you tackle so many? No? Neither can I. We need help from the fine dogs of Houndsville. If we offer free food and a little reward for finding the bracelet, everyone will think it's the most fun they've had in years. I'll ask Dasher Dog to run around and tell everyone."

Duchess Dulay looked at Mr. Bones with a new respect in her eyes. She had never heard him sound so masterful.

And the baker's idea turned out to be an excellent one. Almost all the dogs in Houndsville were happy to accept the invitation that Dasher Dog brought to them—after all, no dog in his right mind would ever turn down the chance to eat Mr. Bones' meat pies.

By lunchtime, several picnic tables in the street outside were groaning with goodies. And several dogs were groaning to get at them, especially in view of the very generous reward offered by Duchess Dulay.

"Just be careful with your teeth!" called Mr. Bones. "Remember that diamonds are very hard!"

And fifteen minutes later, Mr. Bones' idea was rewarded when a great shout went up at one table.

"I've found it!" cried a small poodle called Daphne. And everybody cheered.

Later that day, Duchess Dulay came to thank Mr. Bones for his help.

"Not at all, Duchess," replied the baker, looking flushed. "It was a pleasure."

"Please," said the Duchess, turning pink herself now, "do call me Davina."

"Only if you will call me Barker," said Mr. Bones firmly. "Allow me to escort you home, Davina."

And he offered her his arm.

Mrs. Gruff the Greengrocer Has

A Very Long Rest

Mrs. Gruff the Greengrocer had been feeling very tired recently, and she couldn't imagine why. It was true that she worked every day with her husband in their greengrocer's shop, and the shop was always very busy. In the evening, when she had locked the door behind the last customer, there was clearing up to be done and the day's earnings to be counted.

Of course, there was an early start every morning, too, when Mrs. Gruff went with her husband in their van to pick up fresh fruit and vegetables for the shop.

But Mrs. Gruff had been doing all those things for years, and she had never felt the slightest bit tired. She loved chatting with the customers and finding out about *everything* that was going on in Houndsville.

"Perhaps I'm just getting old," she said to Mr. Gruff one evening, as she put her paws up at last.

"Nonsense, my dear," said that gentleman gallantly, putting on his comfy slippers. But … er … perhaps you're not quite as … er … sylphlike as once you were. Maybe that is making you tired."

Mr. Gruff knew he had made a mistake as soon as the words were out of his mouth.

"You mean I'm *fat*?" cried his wife, rushing to the mirror above the fireplace.

"I can still wear my wedding dress after all these years," cried Mrs. Gruff. "Well, almost."

Mr. Gruff succeeded in calming his wife down at last. He suggested it was time she took a rest from the business for a few days.

"I can ask Spotty Smith to help me out for a day or two," he said. "You just take it easy, my dear. And I will do all the cooking. At least, I'll buy us some delicious meals from Mr. Bones' shop. You won't have to do a thing."

Mrs. Gruff sighed. It was very tempting. She really did feel exhausted, and in fact, although she did not want to admit it to Mr. Gruff, she had found it difficult to button up her clothes recently. A few days of rest, eating healthy things and relaxing, would do her a world of good. It would be like going to a health farm while staying at home.

And Mrs. Gruff really did enjoy her rest. She lay on the sofa and read all the magazines she loved, such as *Hounds Beautiful* and *Pawsmopolitan*.

After a week, Mr. Gruff asked how she was feeling.

"Much better," said his wife. "But I still don't feel quite myself. Maybe a few more days' rest will do the trick."

So when customers inquired about his wife, Mr. Gruff simply said she was still resting.

One day, it was Dr. Fetch who asked. And when he heard the reply, he decided he should see how Mrs. Gruff was for himself.

"A young dog like you shouldn't be feeling tired all the time," he said when he saw her.

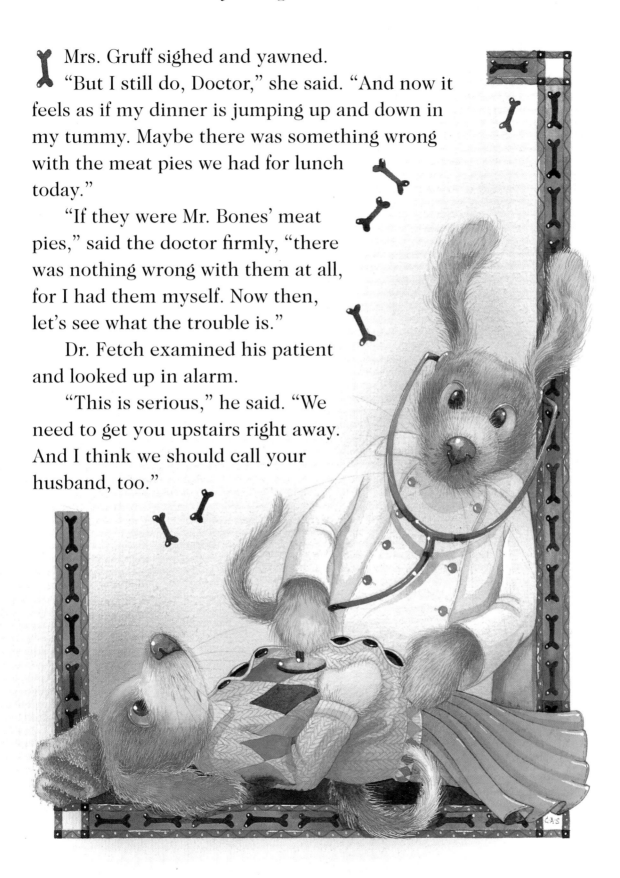

Mrs. Gruff sighed and yawned.

"But I still do, Doctor," she said. "And now it feels as if my dinner is jumping up and down in my tummy. Maybe there was something wrong with the meat pies we had for lunch today."

"If they were Mr. Bones' meat pies," said the doctor firmly, "there was nothing wrong with them at all, for I had them myself. Now then, let's see what the trouble is."

Dr. Fetch examined his patient and looked up in alarm.

"This is serious," he said. "We need to get you upstairs right away. And I think we should call your husband, too."

But Mr. Gruff was busy on the telephone, sorting out a pumpkin problem. It was over an hour later that he was given the message. At once, he left the shop in Spotty's paws and hurried home to see his wife.

Mr. Gruff was panting by the time he reached home. He found the front door open and ran anxiously up the stairs, three at a time. Whatever could be the matter? The doctor's message had sounded urgent.

As he burst into the bedroom, Mr. Gruff had the biggest surprise of his life, for there was his wife, sitting up in bed and looking as proud as a Pekinese. Tucked in beside her were five little puppies, fast asleep.

"But…" cried Mr. Gruff. "But… but… but… why didn't you tell me?"

"I didn't know," smiled his wife. "I was so busy working that I never thought about puppies. Are you pleased?"

"It's the most wonderful surprise I've ever had," gasped Mr. Gruff, giving her a hug. "But I suppose this means you'll be having an even longer rest now?"

"I've been thinking about that," said Mrs. Gruff sweetly. "And I don't think it's fair for me to do all the resting. We can take turns looking after the puppies … I mean resting … on alternate days."

Mr. Gruff agreed at once. But if you've ever had anything to do with young puppies, you'll know there was very little rest for any of the Gruff family for several years to come!

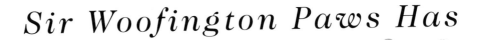

Sir Woofington Paws Has
A Very Wobbly Chimney

Sir Woofington Paws lived in a large house a mile or so from the town of Houndsville. Unfortunately, although his family had once been very wealthy, Sir Woofington was now in reduced circumstances.

This was mostly his father's fault. Old Sir Patchmont Paws had been a great collector. Unfortunately, he hadn't had the vaguest idea what to collect. His famous art collection had turned out to be the work of a small team of professional forgers who could turn their paws to any style or period. Yes, even the famous picture of the Dog's Palace in Venice by Kenneletto was proved to be the work of Towser "The Paintbrush" Terrier, a dog well known to the Pooch Police.

It was the same with Sir Patchmont's collection of fine silver. He had bought it in good faith from a shifty-looking dog who knocked at the door one day. Only a week later, it was discovered that every single piece had been stolen from Duchess Dulay. Of course, it had to be returned.

I need hardly mention what happened to Sir Patchmont's ice-sculpture collection one hot June, or the most unfortunate scene when he discovered two of his nephews munching their way through his very expensive bone collection. It is enough to say that by the time he had finished, Sir Patchmont Paws had lost almost all the family money, leaving his son, Sir Woofington, to try to keep up appearances on a shoestring.

It had once been widely believed in Houndsville that Sir Woofington would marry the widowed Duchess Dulay, but he could not bring himself to propose to her when he had no way of supporting her. So Sir Woofington lived alone in his crumbling home, looking sadly at the spaces on the walls where his father's fake pictures had once hung.

Now Paws Place was literally falling down around Sir Woofington's ears. He couldn't afford to hire professionals to fix his roof or check his plumbing, so he did it himself. Sadly, Sir Woofington's home-improvement skills were dreadfully bad. He frequently made matters worse instead of better.

One morning, Sir Woofington was chopping wood outside the back door when he happened to look up. As he did so, a tiny bird landed on one of the tallest chimneys of the house, and … there could be no doubt about it … it quite distinctly wobbled. The chimney wobbled. The bird wobbled. And Sir Woofington, watching this with a sinking heart, felt his knees wobble too.

I'm afraid that Sir Woofington inherited his brains from his father. Before you could say, "Don't even think about it, Sir W.!" he hurried off to find the very longest ladder in his workshop.

Without waiting for someone to come and help him, Sir Woofington started to climb. Up, up, up he went. And wobble, wobble, wobble went the ladder. Every step brought him nearer to disaster—and every step was wobblier than the one before. But the silly dog kept climbing.

Just as Sir Woofington reached the base of the wobbly chimney, a car drove into his driveway. The climbing dog looked down. As he turned his head, the ladder slipped away, leaving him clinging to the chimney.

Sir Woofington Paws thought his last moments had come. In a faint voice, he called for help. Now that he was close to it, he could see that the chimney was likely to fall down in the slightest breeze. It certainly was not strong enough to support a full-grown dog.

Far below, a dog that Sir Woofington had never seen before looked up in horror at the dangling figure. He spotted a little window not far from Sir Woofington's left paw and, without waiting to knock or introduce himself, he rushed into the house and up the stairs. Just as Sir Woofington felt that he would have to let go, the strange dog grabbed him firmly with a large paw.

Half an hour later, Sir Woofington and his guest were drinking tea in the shabby dining room. (Sir Woofington couldn't afford real houndstooth tea, but his garden was full of nettles.) It was only then, after offering heartfelt thanks, that Sir Woofington asked his visitor why he had come.

To his host's surprise, the large dog flushed pink. "I have come," he said, "to put right a bad thing I did many years ago. When I was a young dog," he went on, "I turned to crime. One day I robbed the home of a rich dog in Houndsville and sold her silver to your father."

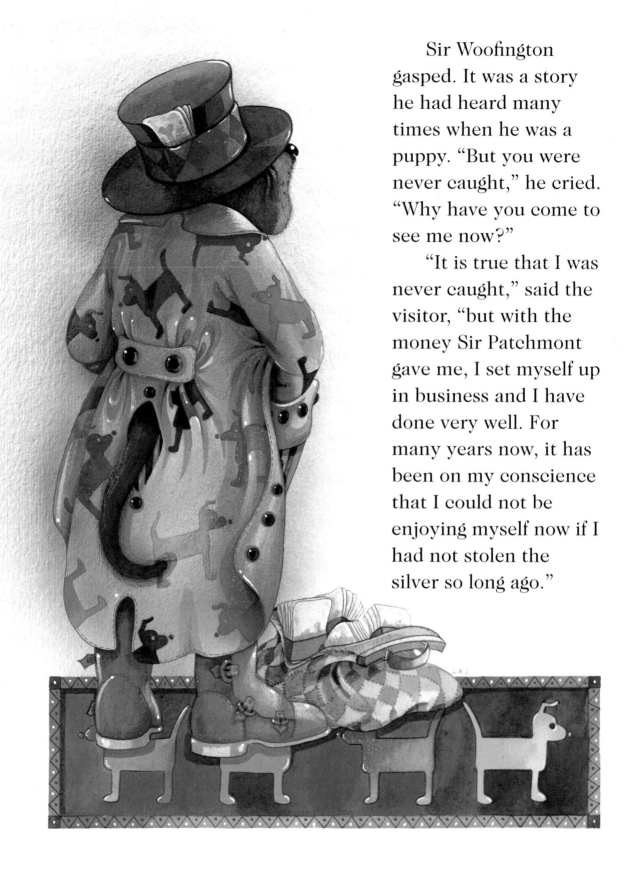

Sir Woofington gasped. It was a story he had heard many times when he was a puppy. "But you were never caught," he cried. "Why have you come to see me now?"

"It is true that I was never caught," said the visitor, "but with the money Sir Patchmont gave me, I set myself up in business and I have done very well. For many years now, it has been on my conscience that I could not be enjoying myself now if I had not stolen the silver so long ago."

"My dear sir," cried Sir Woofington, "this morning you saved my life. What is past is past. I am only too happy to forget the whole thing."

But the stranger shook his head. "You deserve to have half my wealth," he said. "There is plenty for both of us."

So that is how Sir Woofington's fortunes were restored. He is once more seen in the best circles in Houndsville. Paws Place has been repaired by skilled dogs and filled with fine furniture and some (absolutely genuine) pictures. And it is said that Duchess Dulay has been seen dining there recently on more than one occasion!

Mr. Woof the Watchmaker Has

A Very Merry Christmas

When all the dogs of Houndsville are sleeping peacefully in their beds (except Mr. Gruff, who is probably feeding one of his troublesome little puppies), Mr. Woof the Watchmaker is often lying awake, with every hair quivering and his ears twitching eagerly. Is he afraid of things that go bump in the night? No, Mr. Woof is anxious about things that go clang in the night. Or rather, of things that go *clang, dong, ding, bong, ping* in the night!

The poor dog lies there waiting for the clocks in the town to chime. He is dreadfully, dreadfully afraid that one of them will be silent. If it is—and, after all, any clock might go wrong at some time— he fears other dogs will say, "You know, old Woof isn't up to the job any more. He should retire. The church clock has gone wrong three times this year." Mr. Woof doesn't want to retire. He worries about what life might be like without watches to repair and clocks to care for.

Five clocks chime every hour of the day and night in Houndsville—the church clock, the school clock, the Town Hall clock, the station clock, and the clock above Mr. Woof's shop. They all make different sounds, but the old watchmaker recognizes them all. At one o'clock in the morning, he hears them chiming once. *Clang! Dong! Ding! Bong! Ping!* At two o'clock he hears them chime twice. *Clang! Clang! Dong! Dong! Ding! Ding! Bong! Bong! Ping! Ping!* And on it goes.

Even when Mr. Woof finally falls asleep, his
ears are awake, waiting for something to go wrong.

At Christmas, Mr. Woof is even more worried
than usual. If the clocks go wrong, how will the
dogs who sing carols in the town square know
when to begin? How will puppies know when to
open their presents? In fact, how will any dog
know that Christmas has arrived at last?

Now, Mr. Woof's fears
about growing older are not
completely silly. He is not
as lively a dog as he once
was. His paws are not as
nimble, and his eyesight
is not as sharp. He is also
only too aware that his
young nephew, Hunter
Houndly, is building up
a flourishing business
on the other side of town.
Mr. Woof taught Hunter
everything he knows. He
planned that Hunter would
take over his business, but
when the time came, he
found that he just couldn't stop.

Not unreasonably, Hunter pointed out that now that he was trained, he wanted to be a real watchmaker. He had no choice but to open his own shop. Mr. Woof was proud of him, but he was anxious too.

In fact, Mr. Woof was so worried that he had become quite unable to think sensibly about the situation. And the more nights he spent lying awake, the less sensible he was able to be. He was making himself ill, and everyone could see it, but no one could think of a way to bring him to his senses.

At last, though, a snowstorm came to the rescue. It was the worst snowstorm ever to hit Houndsville, and it happened on Christmas Eve. The first flakes began fluttering down in the morning. By the afternoon, it was snowing heavily. By the time darkness fell, traffic could no longer travel on the snow-filled streets of Houndsville. Dogs hurrying home, bundled up against the cold, told each other how lucky it was that the snow had come on Christmas Eve, when everyone wanted to be at home with their families anyway. And, of course, all the little puppies squealed with delight to see their town looking just like an old-fashioned Christmas card.

Mr. Woof heard all the clocks of the town strike six, but the sound was muffled by the snow. He was so tired after he had sold the final last-minute present and closed up his shop that he decided to go straight to bed. He fell asleep at once.

Which is why, some time later, Mr. Woof didn't hear the five clocks striking seven … or eight … or nine. At least, it wasn't because he was asleep that he didn't hear them, but because they didn't strike. Snow had muffled their chimes and clogged up their mechanisms. Every one of them was silent. Mr. Woof slept on.

Christmas Day dawned bright
... and white. Outside, the
whole town sparkled in
the sunshine. Mr. Woof
awoke and knew at once
that something
wonderful had
happened. He had
enjoyed a whole night's
sleep! He felt young and
refreshed! He felt full of
the joys of Christmas! And,
more than anything else, he
felt, now that he could think clearly,
that he had been a very silly dog.
Mr. Woof didn't waste any time. He quickly
wrapped up a very special present and set off for
Hunter Houndly's house.

As he padded
through the snow, he
couldn't help noticing
that the silent clocks had
not stopped any of the
fun in Houndsville. The
singers were howling
their heads off in the
town square. Puppies everywhere were squealing
over their new presents. Everyone looked cheerful.
"Merry Christmas, Mr. Woof!" they called, as he
walked by. Not one of them mentioned the clocks.

Mr. Woof smiled to himself as he reached Hunter Houndly's door and rang the bell. "Season's Greetings, Hunter!" he cried, as his nephew opened the door. "Here's a present for you."

Hunter gasped as he tore off the paper. "It's the key to my shop," confirmed his uncle, "or rather, it's the key to *your* shop. I'm not going to worry about clocks now. Oh, and by the way, I think you should take a look at the clock above the shop. It seems to have stopped. Not a very good advertisement for a watchmaker, is it? Merry Christmas!"

Mrs. Trot the Toy Seller Has
A VERY BIG PROBLEM

One afternoon, Mrs. Trot was just about to close her toyshop for the day when Mrs. Muncher knocked urgently on the door.

"Oh! I am so glad you haven't closed!" she cried. "I have to buy a present for one of the little Gruff puppies. Young George Gruff is my godson, you know, and I promised him a special present if he stopped chewing his daddy's ears. I hear he's been as good as gold this week, so I must keep my promise."

"Of course," agreed Mrs. Trot. "What kind of present did you have in mind?"

"Oh, something small," replied her customer. "In fact, I know just what he would like—a toy elephant. He's got a little book about one, and he really loves it."

Mrs. Trot looked around her shelves. There were toy pandas and giraffes and tigers. There were cuddly polar bears and fluffy zebras. But there were no elephants at all.

"Don't worry!" cried Mrs. Trot. "I can telephone the warehouse in Dogborough and ask them to make an overnight delivery. They supply anything you could ever want. Lots of the shops in town use them. Just leave it to me. If you stop by tomorrow morning, on your way to see young George, I'll have the elephant ready and waiting. I'll even wrap it for you if you like."

"That would be perfect," smiled Mrs. Muncher.

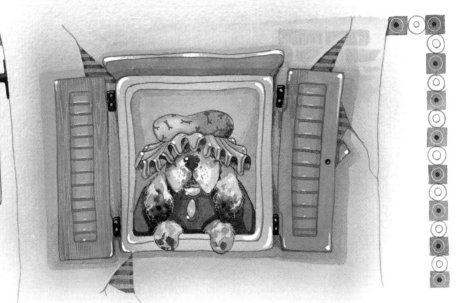

Mrs. Trot was still in bed the next morning when she heard a big truck pull up outside her house. She smiled to herself. Thank goodness for that warehouse. Its deliveries were always reliable. Not wanting to open the door in her nightie, she poked her head out of the window and called to the driver, whom she knew well.

"Just leave it on the doorstep, can you, Dasher? I'll be down in a minute, but I don't want to hold you up."

"No problem!" called the delivery dog. "Shall I tie it to the door knocker, so it doesn't wander off? I've got some strong string in the truck."

But Mrs. Trot's head had disappeared from the window. She was busily getting dressed so she could wrap the toy before Mrs. Muncher arrived.

Dasher shook his head and went to open the doors of the truck.

In fact, Mrs. Trot was not able to get ready as quickly as she had hoped. Just as she was buttoning her skirt, the telephone by her bed rang. It was her cousin, who lived in China!

Of course, Mrs. Trot couldn't just put the phone down. She chatted for a long time, forgetting the package on the doorstep. When she finished at last, she looked at her watch in dismay. Mrs. Muncher was due any minute!

Scuttling down the stairs, Mrs. Trot reached the front door in three seconds flat. She flung open the door and found…

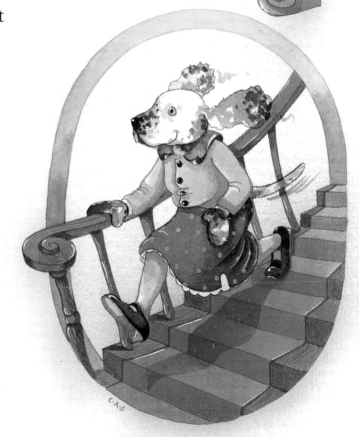

a real elephant!

Just at that moment, Mrs. Muncher arrived.
"I said a *small* present!" she gasped.
"I'm afraid I haven't had time to wrap it," cried
Mrs. Trot.
Then they both started laughing so hard the
tears ran down their whiskers.

Luckily, it didn't take long for the mix-up to be sorted out. Dasher returned with a much smaller elephant and took charge of the larger one.

"I'm sorry," he said. "This fellow was on his way home to India, but the labels must have got mixed up. It's not often we have two elephant deliveries on one day."

Just then, the elephant stuck his trunk into the rain barrel outside Mrs. Trot's shop and did what elephants do. Mrs. Trot and Mrs. Muncher jumped out of the way just in time.

"Never mind!" laughed Mrs. Trot. "My shop window did need washing! It's been a most interesting day so far!"

"And I've got a wonderful story to tell my godson," smiled Mrs. Muncher. "It's much better than the one in his storybook!"

Dasher the Delivery Dog Has A Very Strange Package

asher the Delivery Dog often laughed about the jobs he had to do. It was lucky that he was such a lively, cheerful dog, because his customers were sometimes very difficult. One elderly dog changed her mind three times about where she wanted her new piano—and then sent it back to the shop after all.

In his working life, Dasher had been asked to deliver many strange things, and he always did it with his usual friendly smile, until one day he had a package for the Perfect Poodle Beauty Salon.

The Salon was run by Miss Evangeline Puff, a dog who would never dream of appearing in public without at least seven bows in her hair and probably some frills and ribbons as well.

Before he made a delivery to her shop, Dasher always tried to guess whether today her hair would be pink, or yellow, or blue, or green, or the vivid shade of purple Evangeline chose when she needed cheering up.

On this particular morning, Dasher picked up his packages from the depot as usual and decided to deliver the one for the Perfect Poodle Beauty Salon first, since it was the nearest. He put the package beside him on the seat of his delivery truck and set off. As he did so, Dasher couldn't help noticing that the package had been sent from Brazil, and he gave a little shudder.

What, you may ask, was so terrible about Brazil? It's a wonderful country. But Dasher knew that Brazil had miles and miles of rich, lush, tropical forest. And where there is rich, lush, tropical forest, there are creepy things, and crawly things, and little skittery, nibbling creatures. And where there are *those*, there are sometimes great big red hairy spiders. Dasher wasn't afraid of *anything*—except great big red hairy spiders. The very thought of one of those made him shivery all over.

Dasher knew that Evangeline was not likely to have started ordering spiders for her Salon, but he kept a careful eye on the package all the same.

All went well, until Dasher whizzed around a
corner and found a group of little puppies about to
cross the road with their teacher Mr. Terrier.
Dasher slammed on his brakes and stopped safely,
but as he did so, the package from Brazil flew off
the seat and onto the floor. Dasher waved to Mr.
Terrier and the puppies, then stooped to pick up
the package. The fall had torn the paper a little,
and the string was getting looser and looser by the
second. To Dasher's horror, he distinctly saw some
red hairy stuff poking out of the torn paper—and
it was moving!

As a matter of fact, the package was moving because Dasher's paws were trembling, but he didn't think of that. He slammed the truck into gear and set off the second the puppies were safely across the road.

Poor Dasher really was flustered with fear. He didn't know what to do except drive as quickly as he safely could to Evangeline Puff's Salon. But all the time he was driving, he imagined the biggest, reddest, hairiest spider in the world slowly creeping out of the package beside him. The thought was so very horrible that he didn't even dare to look at the package. He drove with his eyes straight ahead and his paws gripping the wheel as if his life depended on it.

As Mr. Bones told
Duchess Dulay when
they had lunch together
later that day, "Old
Dasher really was
dashing this morning.
And he was in such a
hurry, he didn't even
wave to me."

Waving was the last thing on Dasher's mind.
Any second, he expected to feel a soft touch on his
knee as the spider began to climb across to his
side of the truck.

When Dasher pulled up outside the Perfect
Poodle Beauty Salon, his nerves were at breaking
point. He forgot to guess whether Evangeline
would be blue or pink. He just rushed inside and
flung himself down in a chair.

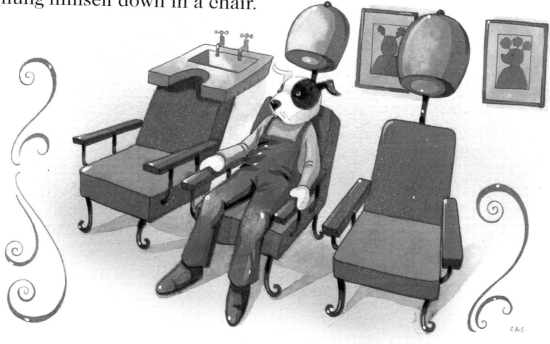

"There's a package for you in my truck," he gasped. "Can you get it, please? I'll just wait right over here and hurry off when you've got it." And he scuttled over to the farthest corner of the Salon.

Evangeline Puff was surprised, but she did what Dasher asked. She read a lot of novels in her spare time, with glamorous heroines and daring heroes. It flashed across her mind that maybe Dasher was being chased by a gang of enemy spies. How exciting!

But outside, she found her package easily and, except for the corner being a little torn, it looked fine.

"I'm so glad this has arrived, Dasher," said Evangline, coming back into her Salon. "Look!"

Dasher almost fainted as Evangline tore open the package to reveal … an amazing red wig with sequins and tropical flowers all over it!

When Dasher had recovered from the shock, he was so relieved he told Evangeline the whole story.

"Poor Dasher," she cried. "Let me give you a special haircut to make you feel better."

But Dasher, looking at the very elaborate hairstyles shown around the walls, said no politely and went on his way. Although there's nothing quite as frightening as a great big red hairy spider from Brazil, let's face it, Evangeline's hairstyles come pretty close!

Mr. Terrier the Teacher Has
A VERY ODD FEELING

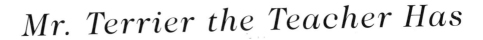

Puppies, as I'm sure you know, can be naughtier than almost any other little animals. They chew things. They sharpen their little claws on things. And when they are very small, I'm afraid they sometimes leave little … er … *puddles* around the place. You can imagine that teaching a whole class of puppies is not an easy job. Mr. Terrier the Teacher felt that he needed five pairs of paws and eyes in the back of his head.

One morning, when Mr. Terrier took off his hat and began to write on the board about the important subject of lampposts and how to use them, he heard a lot of giggling going on at the back of the room.

"Ruffles! Rupert! Randall! Is that you?" he called, knowing that the naughty triplets were often at the bottom of any trouble.

But the three little dogs spoke up at once with solemn faces.

"No, sir!"

"No, sir!"

"No, sir!"

Mr. Terrier frowned and turned back to his writing. But now the giggling was louder than ever. Mr. Terrier spun around as quickly as he could, his ears flying. In fact, he turned so quickly he felt dizzy and had to clutch at his desk.

He was not quick enough. As the room revolved gently around him, all the poor teacher could see was twenty innocent little faces looking up at him. Slowly, he turned back to his work.

This time, the giggling was uncontrolled. When Mr. Terrier turned around, he saw little puppies rolling on the floor with merriment. Some even had tears of laughter dripping from their whiskers.

Mr. Terrier used his iciest tones.

"Would someone please tell me just *what* is so funny? Well? *Oooooh!*"

Just at that moment, Mr. Terrier felt a very odd feeling where his shirt collar met his neck. It was slithery and slimy and squirmy and enough to make even the bravest dog run yelping to his mother. Mr. Terrier would have done just that if it were not for the fact that twenty pairs of naughty eyes were watching him eagerly. And twenty pink tongues were panting with glee.

"Rupert!" called the teacher. "Would you come here a minute, please?" It took all Mr. Terrier's self-control not to start squealing.

Rupert trotted to the front of the class, looking a little apprehensive.

"I wonder," said Mr. Terrier, "if you would mind removing the snake that is wriggling down my neck. I wouldn't want it to get squashed."

Mr. Terrier was determined to remain cool and calm. It would take more than a slithering reptile to frighten *him*.

Rupert looked puzzled.

"There isn't a snake wriggling down your neck, sir," he said. "No snake at all."

"Well, the lizard then," said Mr. Terrier, feeling more uncomfortable by the second, but determined not to show it. "Don't split hairs with me, young puppy."

"There's no lizard either, sir," said Rupert, looking horribly truthful.

"Is it a spider? Is it a worm? Is it a centipede?" asked Mr. Terrier, his voice rising with every question. Then he had an even worse thought. "Is it," he squeaked, "a frog?"

"Sir, are you feeling well?" asked Rupert, looking concerned. "Why don't you sit down? It is hot in here."

Mr. Terrier could feel the slithering and sliding getting worse and worse. He simply couldn't bear it any more. Visions of tarantulas, toads, and things that crawl out from under rocks filled his head. He gave a little cry and pulled off his coat, flinging it on the floor.

From out of the coat, something red and yellow and slimy began to crawl. Mr. Terrier stepped back in horror. Was it some alien life form, ready to take over the world?

But as he looked, horrified, at the horrible stuff, Mr. Terrier's nose began to twitch. When a dog's eyes are playing tricks on him, his nose will often set him straight. And this time, Mr. Terrier's nose was telling him something very strange. It was telling him that the slimy yellow and red crawling stuff was … plums and custard!

Mr. Terrier took a step forward. He looked carefully at the mess on the floor. It smelled like plums and custard. It looked like plums and custard. Mr. Terrier stooped down and put out a cautious paw. He raised the paw to his mouth. There was no doubt about it, it *was* plums and custard! Lots of it!

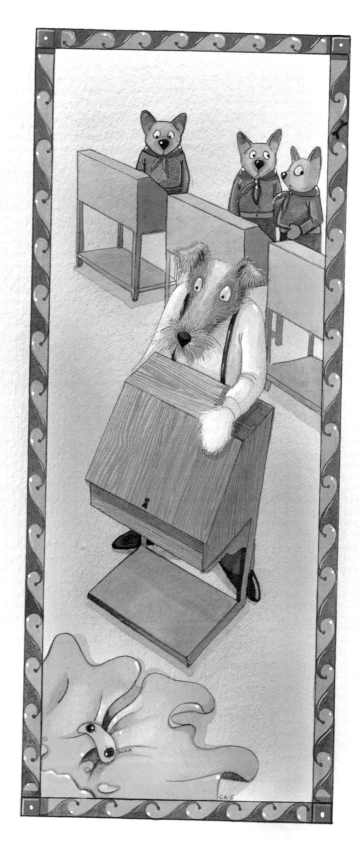

Mr. Terrier was angry. He was very angry indeed. Wiping the back of his neck with his handkerchief as best he could, he faced the class.

"Which of you naughty, nasty, *silly* little puppies has done this?" he asked. "And," he went on, as a thought struck him, "how?"

Mr. Terrier looked at the ceiling for a hanging bucket of dripping custard. There wasn't one.

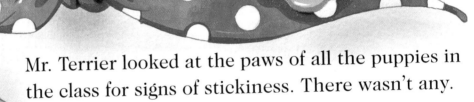

Mr. Terrier looked at the paws of all the puppies in the class for signs of stickiness. There wasn't any.

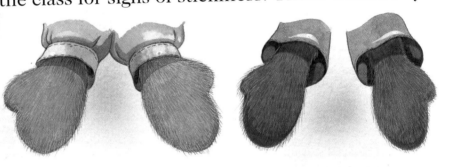

Mr. Terrier looked under desks and inside schoolbags for spoons or bowls or cartons. There weren't any.

And then, at the back of Mr. Terrier's mind, there came a little whispering thought. It told him his elderly mother had been making supper last night. It told him she had been called to the telephone just as she was pouring something into a big bowl. It told him that, as he handed her the telephone, he had also put his hat down on the table. It also told him he had rushed to work this morning without stopping to think about anything, even the slightly strange way his hat felt as it sat on his head.

"Puppies!" said Mr. Terrier. "I owe you an apology. I know now that you did not put snakes, or lizards, or worms, or frogs, or tarantulas, or plums and custard on my head or down my back. The culprit … and I will not hesitate to name him … was … ME! Sometimes old dogs can be as silly as young ones. Now I must go and clean myself up."

And it is an even stranger thing that all those puppies liked Mr. Terrier a lot more after that, and they were never as naughty again.

Old Mrs. Merrypaws Has A Very Welcome Visitor

Houndsville is a wonderful place to live. The summers are hot and sunny. The winters are cold and snowy. But just sometimes, in that in-between time that is not quite winter and not quite spring, there is rain … and more rain … and even more rain for day after day after day.

Mrs. Merrypaws looked out of her window one day and saw dark clouds above the trees beside the road. She shook her head anxiously.

"Only once in my life have I seen clouds like that," she told Mr. Clipped next door. "That was before the Great Flood."

Mr. Clipped shuddered. The Great Flood was before his time, but he had heard older dogs talking about it. He decided there and then to visit his sister a hundred miles away.

Mrs. Merrypaws decided she must be prepared for the worst. She began to make lists of the things she would need: food—lots of it—in cans and jars and waterproof packages; warm, waterproof clothes; sandbags to stop the water from coming in under the front door; a small inflatable boat if the worst came to the worst. For Mrs. Merrypaws felt that she was too old to swim to safety these days.

No sooner had Mrs. Merrypaws made her arrangements than it started to rain.

"Just as I thought," she said, looking out at the puddles on her path. "It won't be long now."

That night, Mrs. Merrypaws was well prepared when she went to bed. She had all her provisions and emergency equipment piled around her bed. In fact, it was piled so high, she couldn't see out of the window.

"I'm going to take a long, hot bath before bed," said the old dog to herself. "It may be the last one I can have for some time."

Later, tucked in her bed, Mrs. Merrypaws heard the howling of the wind and the lashing of the rain on the window as she closed her eyes.

Next morning, Mrs. Merrypaws woke to the sound of the swish-swash of water. She put one paw out of bed as usual and felt for her slipper. Instead, her toes touched something cold and wet. Peering over the edge of her bed, she saw to her horror that there was water all around!

"If there is water up here, the whole ground floor of the house must be flooded already!" said Mrs. Merrypaws. "Thank goodness I brought everything up here last night!"

Just then, a cheery voice called from the window. "Granny! Are you all right?"

It was Gerry, Mrs. Merrypaws' grandson. "Wait a moment!" called Mrs. Merrypaws, wading across the floor. But when she reached the window at last, she found to her astonishment that Gerry was not in a boat but up a ladder!

"You didn't hear me downstairs," he explained, "so I thought I'd check that you were all right."

Mrs. Merrypaws stared in disbelief at the scene outside the window. The sun was shining. There was not a puddle on the path. Then she looked at the scene inside. The sound of rushing water could still be heard, but now, suddenly, it sounded suspiciously like an overflowing bathtub.

"I'll be down in a minute," she told Gerry. "But in the meantime, let me give you some advice. If you worry too much about what *might* happen, you might not notice what *is* happening in front of your nose."

Young Gerry never did really understand what she was talking about, but I think we do, don't we?

Mr. Wag the Window Cleaner Has
A Very Shaky Start

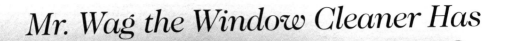

No wonder the windows in Houndsville are so bright and shining. Every day, Mr. Wag the Window Cleaner is up on his ladder, working hard.

Now window cleaners, as I'm sure you know, see all kinds of things as they go about their business. It's hard not to notice what is happening on the other side of a sheet of glass—especially when it is extra clean! But Mr. Wag had a very strict rule: he never, ever gossiped about what he saw. He just tried to forget he had ever seen it.

It was on a sunny morning in early summer that Mr. Wag's rule was tested to its limits. He'd just arrived to clean Duchess Dulay's windows when he met Mr. Bones on the doorstep.

Mr. Bones, usually a most polite and courteous dog, barely said hello. He was nervously squashing his hat between his paws and clutching a large bouquet of flowers under his arm.

Mr. Wag smiled knowingly. It was well known that Duchess Dulay had recently hired a very pretty cook. No doubt Mr. Bones had come to call on her.

Mr. Wag climbed his ladder and began work on the living room windows. He was too busy to notice what was going on inside, and had just begun to slosh on the water, when he suddenly heard a scream.

"Oooooerrrrr!" Mr. Wag grabbed desperately at the window as his ladder wobbled alarmingly. Then, still somewhat shaken, Mr. Wag peered through the glass.

Inside, he saw Duchess Dulay ... and Mr. Bones. And ... oh, my goodness! ... Mr. Bones seemed to be strangling her!

Mr. Wag didn't hesitate. He dropped his bucket to the ground far below and flung open the window. Then he hurled himself into the room.

"What's going on here?" he cried loudly, as he landed with a thump on the living room carpet.

"I beg your pardon!" gasped Duchess Dulay in horror. "What is the meaning of this?"

It was only then that Mr. Wag suddenly realized that Mr. Bones hadn't been strangling Duchess Dulay at all. He had been kissing her! And what was more, Duchess Dulay had been kissing him right back!

Mr. Wag wished the floor would open up and swallow him. He had broken a window. He had made a complete fool of himself. And he had probably lost two of his very best customers. Mumbling miserably, he tried to explain.

But the Duchess was smiling, and Mr. Bones stepped forward.

"This has been a very eventful morning," he said. "Mr. Wag, I would like to be the first to introduce you to the future Mrs. Bones."

"Oh, Barker," sighed the Duchess, "you always know *exactly* the right thing to say!"

A VERY FAMOUS CUSTOMER

Miss Bark loved working in her bookshop. It wasn't because she had lots of customers and made a good living. In fact, she had very few customers and had been known to give books away to dogs she thought would like them. No, what Miss Bark loved about her shop was that it gave her the chance to *read* all day. From morning until night, she sat in her comfy armchair and read all the books she liked best—and that was usually detective stories, the more complicated the better.

The books Miss Bark loved best of all were the Bloodhound Bungay stories by D. O. Gnaw. In these a bloodhound (of course), called Bungay (of course), *always* caught the criminal (of course)!

One morning, Miss Bark had just reached the most exciting part of a Bloodhound Bungay mystery called *The Hidden Pawprint*, when the shop doorbell rang.

"Bother!" said Miss Bark, under her breath. But she hurried forward anyway.

"Can I help you, sir?" she asked the tall, distinguished-looking dog who had just entered.

You can imagine how surprised she was when the visitor replied, "Yes. Do you have any of the works of D. O. Gnaw? I am referring to the Bloodhound Bungay stories, of course."

"I have all of them!" cried Miss Bark. "Every one from *The Mysterious Matter of the Tail that Wagged* to *Bungay's Final Case.*"

"Ah," said the customer, "that is excellent, but it is one book in particular I am looking for. I used to have a copy, but I lost it. I know it is not being printed any longer and very hard to find. It is called *The Hidden Pawprint*. I am willing to pay a large sum of money for it."

Poor Miss Bark was terribly torn. On the one paw, she badly needed some money to repair the heating system before winter arrived. On the other paw, she had only one precious copy of that book herself—and she hadn't finished reading it!

Miss Bark felt desperate. She simply couldn't make up her mind what to do. At last, she found herself telling her customer about her problem!

The customer smiled. "If you have reached the exciting part, you must be near the end," he said. "What if I sat down here and waited for you to finish? Then you could sell me the book."

So Miss Bark supplied him with a cup of coffee and a comfy chair and went back to reading her book. Almost an hour later, she closed it with a snap and a satisfied sigh.

"It was excellent," she said. "And I didn't guess the criminal until two pages before the end."

"Praise indeed," smiled the customer, as he put the book into his pocket and handed over a really very large sum of money.

Miss Bark thought that was the end of the matter. Then, almost a year later, a package arrived for her. Inside was a copy of a brand new edition of *The Hidden Pawprint*!

Miss Bark stared in disbelief at the first page of the book. It said:

DEDICATED TO MISS BARK,
MY MOST DEVOTED READER

As Miss Bark's paws trembled, a small piece of paper fluttered to the ground. She has kept it to this day:

My publisher needed a copy to print this new edition, and you were kind enough to find me one. I hope you enjoy it just as much the second time around.
With grateful thanks,
D. O. Gnaw

Miss Dig the Dressmaker Has
A Very Scary Night

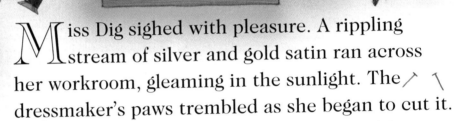

Miss Dig sighed with pleasure. A rippling stream of silver and gold satin ran across her workroom, gleaming in the sunlight. The dressmaker's paws trembled as she began to cut it.

The satin was for Duchess Dulay's wedding dress, and the wedding was only days away. Miss Dig worked on, late into the night.

Miss Dig was young and enthusiastic, but she had been up since dawn. As the summer moon rose in the sky, her head drooped and she fell asleep right there in the workroom, surrounded by a sea of silver and gold.

It was midnight when the church clock's clanging caused Miss Dig to stir. As she opened her sleepy eyes, she saw a horrifying sight. Coming toward her, billowing in the breeze from the open window, was a gruesome shape. It seemed to glow and shimmer as it moved, looking like no dog she had ever seen.

Miss Dig was too frightened even to howl. The eerie chiming of the clock seemed to fill her head. And still the shining figure came forward. With a little gasp, Miss Dig grasped a vase of flowers from the table and flung it at the shape ... which collapsed on the floor.

It was only then Miss Dig saw that it was just some of the Duchess's satin, blown by the breeze. But what had she done? Across the fabric was a huge stain, where water from the vase had soaked into it. There was nothing the poor dog could do—except wait for the water to dry and see if the stain showed.

Miss Dig went to bed. She didn't expect to sleep, but she did. In the morning, she came down to the workroom, clasping her paws together to stop them from shaking.

There lay the silver and gold satin, shining in the sunlight once more. It looked perfect. Miss Dig sighed and smiled. Of the two frights of the past few hours, the second had been much worse than the first. It certainly had been a very scary night.

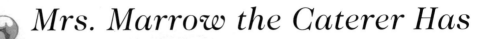

Mrs. Marrow the Caterer Has

A VERY SPECIAL JOB

Catering for a wedding at which two hundred of the top dogs in the area will be present is hard enough, but when the bridegroom is himself a famous and well-loved baker, the job becomes very difficult indeed.

Poor Mrs. Marrow was used to supplying food for big occasions. She was not used to having Mr. Bones peering over her shoulder every five minutes. He was a kind dog, but he was, naturally, nervous about his wedding. He so wanted everything to be perfect.

"Oh, Mrs. Marrow," he would say, "are you sure a bone soufflé is a good idea? The young puppies will make such a mess on the carpets. All the Gruff little ones are bridesmaids and pages, you know."

"It will be wonderful," said Mrs. Marrow firmly.

"And will the cake be finished in time?"

"It will be wonderful," said the caterer.

"Do you think the food will still look attractive with all those flowers around it?"

"It will be wonderful," smiled Mrs. Marrow.

As you can tell by now, Mrs. Marrow had one reply for all questions. It made Mr. Bones worry even more. Did she really know what she was doing? He decided to set a little trap.

"Mrs. Marrow," he cried, "I've decided after all to use black tablecloths and plastic spoons. Do you think that will be all right?"

"It will be wonderful," said Mrs. Marrow.

Now Mr. Bones was dreadfully worried. In fact, he was so concerned about the catering, he almost forgot to get ready for the wedding, and Dasher the Delivery Dog had to dash as he had never dashed before to get him to the church on time.

But the moment Mr. Bones saw Duchess Dulay in her beautiful dress, all his worries disappeared.

"Do you promise to love her and help her to the end of your days?" asked the priest, and Mr. Bones forgot himself entirely.

"It will be wonderful," he sighed.

It certainly was the most beautiful wedding ever seen in Houndsville—and there's no need to worry, the food was wonderful, too!